For all the children who stay in the shade
with their socks on

Rabén & Sjögren Bokförlag, Stockholm
http://www.raben.se

Translation copyright © 2002 by Rabén & Sjögren Bokförlag
All rights reserved
Originally published in Sweden by Rabén & Sjögren under the title
Gittan och fårskallarna
Copyright © 2001 by Pija Lindenbaum
Library of Congress Control Number: 2001098270
Printed in Denmark
First American edition, 2002
ISBN 91-29-65650-8

Rabén & Sjögren Bokförlag is part of
P. A. Norstedt & Söner Publishing Group, established in 1823

BRIDGET
and the
Muttonheads

Pija Lindenbaum

Translated by Kjersti Board

R&S
BOOKS

Stockholm   New York   London   Adelaide   Toronto

Bridget is not at home.
For several days now, she has been
living in a house called the Hotel.
There are no children there, and
no sandbox—only grownups who
talk strangely and wear bathing
suits all day long.

It is hot at the hotel.
It is hot no matter what you do.
"Come on, jump in," says Bridget's mother.
"ALL children love to swim!" says her father.
But Bridget doesn't think that is necessary.
She is fine in her chair.
Besides, she would rather be digging in the sand.
"We are on vacation, sweetheart," her mother
says. "You don't need any sand.
We are here to sit in the sun and go swimming!"

A man comes running.
"SPLISH! SPLASH! KABOOM!" he yells
and does a cannonball into the water.

Bridget doesn't like men who splash.
So she goes off somewhere else.
Only Bridget's wet bathing suit is left.
Mom and Dad are very happy.
They think that Bridget has been
swimming.

Behind the hotel, Bridget finds a path
that disappears into the bushes.
There is sand on the other side of the bushes!
Bridget digs marvelous tunnels for moles
to crawl through. She makes a canal for cargo
ships. And little holes for mermaids to rest in.

When Bridget looks out over the water, she
spots a little island. Little fluffy clouds are
resting on the beach. Bridget keeps on digging,
but she can't help wondering about the clouds
on the island.

Carefully she wades across, making
sure that she doesn't bump into any fish.

On the sand, five sheep lie panting in
the sun, all limp and perspiring heavily.
They make a sound like, "Psst, psst."
"Poor sheep!" Bridget says. "Right in
the full sun, and with so much on!"
Bridget dips the sheep in the water . . .

. . . and then she puts them out to dry in the shade.

Slowly they open their little mouths and whisper, "Biddle-paddle, putty-putty."
Bridget thinks it sounds nice. But she can't really understand them.

When the sheep have dried off and are fluffy once more, they start tramping around in the sand. But they are walking very strangely.

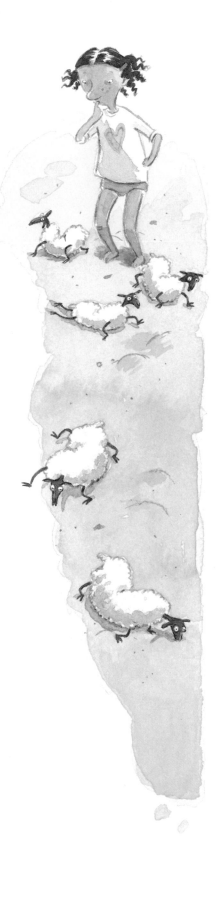

"I guess you need milking,"
Bridget says.
"Pirry-pirry-ho-ho," the sheep answer.
This means, "You'll find some little pails
among the bushes."
Bridget goes to get the pails, and then she
milks the sheep until they are able to walk
normally again. She drinks the milk to be polite.
It tastes terrible, but she doesn't tell them that.

"Hoolim-schoolim," the sheep bleat, sniffing the
air because now they want to look for food.
"I'll help you," says Bridget. "I know what
sheep like."
But there is almost nothing left on the bushes
except thorns. The sheep start sniffing around in
the sand instead. They love lemon soda, cookies,
and old Band-Aids.

sniff-
sniff

The sheep are ravenous and
root around like crazy.
They are really good, Bridget thinks,
and they don't even need shovels!
They don't miss a single crumb.

The sheep gobble up some pieces of cookie
and a sandy apricot that Bridget has found.
Then there is not one drop of lemon soda
or cookie crumb left on the entire island.
But the sheep still want more.
"Hoolim-schoolim," they bleat.
"There is no more food here," Bridget says.
"Why don't you swim across to the other
side? You'll find LOTS to eat there!"

At that, the sheep hide themselves because they don't want to get wet. "Silly little sheep, I can see your noses!" Bridget cries and pulls them out of the sand.

"Now, don't be difficult," she says.

"All sheep know how to swim!"

But the sheep quickly disappear again. That's how
scared they are of fish bumping into their legs.
Bridget looks for them everywhere.
At last she hears some whispering sounds from
the bushes.

"Do you want to stay hungry ALL YOUR LIFE?"
she says and carries the sheep down to the water.
That makes them worried, and they finally do as
she tells them.

Bridget demonstrates the arm strokes.
"Out-and-together, out-and-together," she cries.
Waving your arms around looks like good fun,
the sheep think.
They practice out-and-together for a long time.

Before long, they know what to do with
their legs, too. Then they pretend they are
boiling teapots and blow big bubbles.
They also practice floating.
"Butts in the air!" Bridget cries
as they take off for the other shore.
"That wasn't too bad, was it?" Bridget says.
"Yom-yom," they laugh.

As soon as they have crawled ashore on
the other side, the sheep start panting from
the heat again.

"Wait here!" Bridget cries.
She runs up to the Hotel to get her scissors.

She cuts almost all the fluff off. The sheep
feel cool, and they get nice hairstyles.
She puts the fluff in the mermaid holes
to make them cozy.

Finally Bridget fixes some clothing for the sheep—just in case it gets cold.
She also gives the sheep a whole box of Band-Aids. But the sheep don't like unused Band-Aids. They eat only used ones.
"Silly muttonheads," Bridget says.
"I'll be going home soon. What will happen to you then?"
"Scuttny-huttny," the sheep bleat.
"Oh, good," she says. "Other children can milk you then."
Bridget kisses their dry noses. Then the sheep don't have time for her anymore.

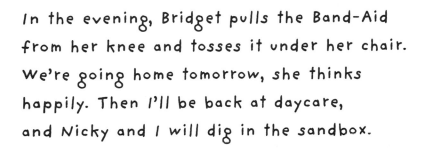

In the evening, Bridget pulls the Band-Aid
from her knee and tosses it under her chair.
We're going home tomorrow, she thinks
happily. Then I'll be back at daycare,
and Nicky and I will dig in the sandbox.

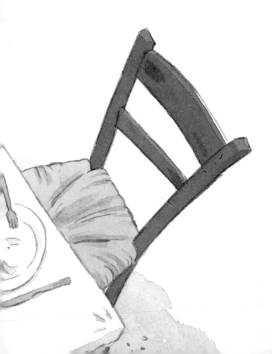

THE END